Anansi
and His Children

Retold by **Bonnie Dobkin**
Illustrated by **Mayur Saikia**

 TeachingStrategies· · Bethesda, MD

For Teaching Strategies, LLC.
Publisher: Larry Bram
Editorial Director: Hilary Parrish Nelson
VP Curriculum and Assessment: Cate Heroman
Product Manager: Kai-leé Berke
Book Development Team: Sherrie Rudick and Jan Greenberg
Project Manager: Jo A. Wilson

For Q2AMedia
Editorial Director: Bonnie Dobkin
Editor and Curriculum Adviser: Suzanne Barchers
Program Manager: Gayatri Singh
Creative Director: Simmi Sikka
Project Manager: Santosh Vasudevan
Illustrator: Mayur Saikia
Designer: Neha Kaul

Teaching Strategies, LLC.
Bethesda, MD
www.TeachingStrategies.com

ISBN: 978-1-60617-139-4

Library of Congress Cataloging-in-Publication Data
Dobkin, Bonnie.
  Anansi and his children / retold by Bonnie Dobkin ; illustrated by Mayur Saikia.
     p. cm.
  Summary: After finding a strange glowing orb in the forest, Anansi the spider puts
    his six clever children to a test to see which one will earn it as a reward.
  ISBN 978-1-60617-139-4
1. Anansi (Legendary character)--Legends. [1. Anansi (Legendary character)--Legends. 2.
Moon--Folklore. 3. Folklore--Africa, West.] I. Saikia, Mayur, ill. II. Title.
  PZ8.1.D674An 2010
  398.20966'0454--dc22
                          2009036448

CPSIA tracking label information:
RR Donnelley, Shenzhen, China
Date of Production: March 2018
Cohort: Batch 6

Printed and bound in China

8 9 10 11	18
Printing	Year Printed

Far, far away, in the land of
the Ashanti, there once lived
a most marvelous creature.
His name was Anansi, and
he was a spider.

Some said Anansi was wise. After all, he had lived a long time and was great friends with Nyame, the God of All Things.

Some said Anansi was clever. After all, he could weave marvelous webs and spin magical stories.

Some said Anansi was a mischief-maker. After all, he loved to play tricks on both enemies and friends, and sometimes on his own family. The truth was, Anansi was all of these things. He was wise and he was clever and he was a mischief-maker!

But Anansi was also a father, and he had six children whom he loved very much. Each had a name that described a special talent.

The first child was called See Trouble, because that's what he could do.

The second child was Road Builder. She could build paths through and to anything.

The third child was River Drinker. He could drain a river down to its rocky bottom.

The fourth child was Game Skinner. No matter what animal he fought, he won.

The fifth child was Stone Thrower. She could pick up a stone, no matter how large, then throw it far and high.

And the sixth child was called Cushion because he was very, very soft.

One day, Anansi found a strange glowing orb in the forest. "How beautiful!" he said. "I will give it to one of my children. But who?" He thought and thought.

"I know," said clever Anansi. "I will go far away, and my children will think I'm lost. Whoever loves me most will come to find me. And that child will receive the orb."

So, Anansi set off. But before he had gone far, Wind came rushing across the plains. He picked Anansi up and spun him through the air, with all his eight legs twirling.

"Ho-ho, Anansi," said Wind. "It's time somebody played a trick on you!"

Wind took Anansi across the plains, through a forest, and over a mountain. Then he dropped Anansi by the side of a river.

"Goodbye, Anansi!" laughed Wind. "Have a nice walk home!"

But Anansi was very dizzy from the spinning and twirling. Before he knew it, he tumbled into the river!

"Oh, no!" said Anansi, rowing with all his eight legs to get back to shore. But before he could reach land, a big fish saw him wriggling, swam up, and swallowed him!

Back at home, See Trouble
saw what had happened.

"Father is in trouble!" he cried.
"We must go and save him!"

Road Builder hopped into action.
She spun a path across the plains,
through the forest, over the mountain,
and to the river.

Now River Drinker went
to work, draining the water.
Soon the fish was flopping
on the rocky bottom.

Next Game Skinner split the fish
wide open. Out popped Anansi!
"My wonderful children!" he cried.

But before he could hug them with any of his eight legs, a falcon swooped down from the sky.

"Not again!" cried Anansi as he was carried into the air.

Now it was Stone Thrower's turn. She snatched up a heavy stone and threw it with all her might.

The stone hit the bird, who screeched and squawked and dropped Anansi.

Cushion scrambled underneath to protect his father from the fall.

19

What a happy tangle there was as Anansi hugged his children with all his eight legs! But then Anansi realized he had a problem. Whom would he give the orb to?

He called out to Nyame, the God of All Things. "Help me, Nyame! Whom shall I choose? After all…

See Trouble saw my danger and called for help.

Road Builder brought my children to me.

River Drinker drained the river that hid me.

Game Skinner opened the fish that swallowed me.

Stone Thrower saved me from the bird's claws.

And Cushion caught me when I fell."

Wise Nyame answered: "Then all your children deserve the treasure. Give the orb to me.

I will place it in the sky for all of them to enjoy."

And the moon is still there,
to this very day.